W9-BSE-258

For Rosa

ALADDIN

An imprint of Simon & Schuster Children's Publishing Division
1230 Avenue of the Americas, New York, New York 10020
This Aladdin hardcover edition December 2017
Text and illustrations copyright © 2011 by Sue Hendra
By Paul Linnet and Sue Hendra
Originally published in Great Britain in 2011 by Simon & Schuster UK Ltd
Published by arrangement with Simon & Schuster UK Ltd
All rights reserved, including the right of reproduction
in whole or in part in any form.
ALADDIN and related logo are registered trademarks of Simon & Schuster, Inc.
For information about special discounts for bulk purchases,
please contact Simon & Schuster Special Sales at 1-866-506-1949
or business@simonandschuster.com.
The Simon & Schuster Speakers Bureau can bring authors to
your live event. For more information or to book an event contact
the Simon & Schuster Speakers Bureau at 1-866-248-3049 or
visit our website at www.simonspeakers.com.
The text of this book was set in Happyjamas.
Manufactured in China 0620 SCP
2 4 6 8 10 9 7 5 3
Library of Congress Control Number 2016959118
ISBN 978-1-4814-9032-0 (hc)
ISBN 978-1-4814-9034-4 (eBook)

NORMAN
THE SLUG WITH THE SILLY SHELL

by Sue Hendra

ALADDIN
New York   London
Toronto   Sydney   New Delhi

Norman the slug thought snails were great.
"Wow!" said Norman. "Look at them! They're amazing!"

But, unfortunately, the snails didn't think
Norman was great.

WHEE!

CRASH!

"Norman, you silly slug!" they cried. "You've spoiled our fun. This only works if you've got a shell."

Norman felt left out. Sadly, he skulked off into the moonlight.

"If only I had a shell of my own," he sighed,
looking at his reflection.

And that's when he had an idea!
"Maybe I could have a shell after all,"
he thought.

But finding a shell was not as easy
as it seemed.

One was too bouncy,

one was too
NOISY,

and one was already taken!

Norman needed time to think. . . . .

Ta-da!
A shell!

It was perfect!

Norman had never been happier.
He could join the snails at last.

Norman LOVED being a snail.

And the snails LOVED Norman's silly shell.

But the fun didn't last for long.

Suddenly, there was a loud flapping of wings.

"Look out! Bird!" cried the snails in panic. "Quick, slither for your lives or we'll end up as supper!"

But the bird was more interested in Norman's silly shell—it looked DELICIOUS!

Norman was being carried up, up, and away, higher and higher into the sky.

What could he do?

Norman did the only thing a slug could do.
He made slime—lots and lots of it!

With a slither and a slother, a slip and a slide,
Norman was FREE!

But he was falling

faster and

faster and

FASTER until . . .

PLONK!

"Norman, Norman, are you okay?" asked the snails.

"Wow!" said Norman. "That was great.
I LOVE flying. If only I had wings. . . ."

Ta-da!

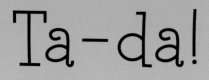